A Gift for a Special Dad:

From:

_____

Occasion:

_____

Date:

_____

A cheerful heart is good medicine.

KING SOLOMON, PROVERBS 17:22

Smiles

for Dads

MARK GILROY
COMMUNICATIONS

Smiles for Dads™

Published by Mark Gilroy Communications, Inc.,
6528 E. 101st Street, Suite 416, Tulsa, Oklahoma 74133-6754
www.markgilroy.com

Design By Jacksondesignco, llc, Siloam Springs, Arkansas

Illustrated by Abbi J. Brown, England, Copyright © 2004

Written by: Nancy B. Gibbs and Christy Philippe, with Jay Cookingham and Tabbitha Easley

ISBN 0-9721682-4-9

Printed in Hong Kong

Smile. . .You're a Dad

Smiles for Dads is ice cold lemonade on a scorching hot day. . .an unexpected bonus on the paycheck before vacation. . .a huge come-from-behind victory by the home team. . .making par on the longest hole on the course. . . sleeping in on Saturday morning. . .a long talk and prayer with your child before turning the lights out.

Through entertaining stories, inspirational quotes and verses, and simple affirmations, let Smiles for Dads provide you with fresh reminders of the joys of being a father.

Rediscover the countless reasons you can raise your children with faith and optimism, and of course, a smile on your face!

My Daddy!

I love these little people; and it is not a slight thing
when they, who are so fresh from God, love us.

CHARLES DICKENS

6

When his mother remarried, the three-year-old boy was thrilled. He adored his new father, a kind man, who was the pastor of their church. About a month after his mom and new dad united in matrimony, the father conducted a formal wedding ceremony.

The young boy sat between his mother and new grandfather, as the young couple repeated their vows.

"What's my new daddy doing, Papa?" the boy asked his grandfather.

"He is marrying the couple up there with him," Papa explained.

With tears in his eyes the young man protested, "But my daddy can't marry them. He just married my mother."

A loving father is the smile that lives in a child's heart.

Frog Patrol

It's never too late to have a happy childhood.

TOM ROBBINS

The little girl dearly loved the creatures of the wild. Her house sat across the street from a pond. A creek ran beside her house. Each afternoon, she searched for frogs and turtles. They became some of her best friends.

Every spring, there were baby frogs everywhere. Once they began hopping, many were killed trying to cross the street. The little girl frantically tried to rescue them early each morning.

One night her father, who saw how upset she was getting, had a talk with her. "You can't save all the frogs," he explained. He let her know how proud he was that she was trying so hard. She wasn't taking his words to heart.

And true enough, the next morning, she was up early to save as many frogs as she could. But she wasn't alone. To her amazement and joy, her father got up early, and in dress slacks and shirt, scurried back and forth across the street to help her return baby frogs to the safety of the pond.

Together, they formed the early morning frog patrol.

Helping our children with the things that matter most to them brings a smile to their face—and ours.

A Walk in the Woods

Trust in the Lord with all your heart and lean not on your own understanding; in all your ways acknowledge him, and he will make your paths straight.

PROVERBS 3:5-6

A father once took his little son for a walk in the woods. As they were tromping along hand in hand, they stopped for a moment, and the father asked, "Do you know where we are?"

The little boy said, "No!"

"Do you know where we're going?" the father asked.

Again, the little boy said, "No!"

The father chuckled and said, "Well, I guess you're lost then!"

The boy looked up at his father and said, "No, I'm not lost. I'm with you!"

A father's presence brings peace to a child's heart.

The Language of Love

We were gentle among you, like a
mother caring for her little children.

1 Thessalonians 2:7

Author Leo Buscaglia told about a contest he was asked to judge. The purpose of the contest was to find the most caring child.

The winner was a four-year-old child whose next-door neighbor was an elderly gentleman who had recently lost his wife. Upon seeing the man cry, the little boy went into the old gentleman's yard, climbed onto his lap, and just sat there.

When his parents asked him what he had said to the neighbor, the little boy said, "Nothing, I just helped him cry."

Your child will teach you life lessons
that make your heart smile.

A Half Dollar Bill

God loves a cheerful giver.

2 CORINTHIANS 9:7

The young family of five filled up half a pew each Sunday morning during worship service at their church. One of their rituals was for the father to give each of his children a crisp, new one dollar bill to put in the collection plate when the offering was taken.

One Sunday, their five-year-old son, Joey, brought his best friend, Thad, to church. The father had not put enough singles in his wallet to give a bill to Thad, and was hoping the young boy wouldn't notice.

As the offering plate was passed toward the family, the father looked down the row to his left. To his surprise and joy, he saw Joey, without a second thought, tear his crisp dollar bill in half and then hand a "half dollar" to Thad to place in the plate.

When dads plant seeds of generosity in their children—
the return on investment is always filled with joy.

"I'm Home"

There is no place more delightful than home.

CICERO

*M*oving day had arrived; a day the middle aged father and mother had dreaded for a long time. They would be moving their youngest child, their only daughter to a distant city to attend college.

Once everything was unloaded and placed in the new apartment, the sad dad and mom said goodbye and quickly left. Neither—especially him—wanted their daughter to see them crying. They drove the 110 miles back home in silence. Once there, the sad couple still exchanged very few words.

A couple hours later, they heard the backdoor open. "I'm home," their daughter shouted.

Mom and Dad both jumped up and ran to greet her, exclaiming, "What are you doing here?"

"I was already homesick and thought I'd visit," she answered with a laugh and a hug.

Mom cried, but the dad had to laugh, realizing his daughter's heart would always reside at home.

Home is where we hang our memories.

No Wasted Days

*Could I climb to the highest place in Athens, I would
lift my voice and proclaim—fellow-citizens, why do ye turn and
scrape every stone to gather wealth, and take so little care of your
children, to whom one day you must relinquish it all?*

SOCRATES

In his advanced years, James Boswell, the renowned 18th Century English writer and biographer of Samuel Johnson, reflected on the most important day of his life. He said it occurred one day during his youth, when his father had invited him to go fishing.

While most of his childhood days had long since been forgotten, during that one day, Boswell said that he had actually learned about what life was all about through the stories his dad told him.

An industrious historian decided to track down the diary of Boswell's father to see how he had reflected on that most important day in the life of his famous son. The entry read: "Went fishing today with my son. A whole day wasted."

He could not have been more wrong. And we can be sure that neither will we always recognize the moments when we made the biggest difference in our children's lives.

Time invested in the lives of your children is never wasted.

Letting Go

Children are not things to be molded,
but people to be unfolded.

JESS LAIR

Craig's son, Joey, was eagerly looking forward to the birthday party of a friend who lived only a few blocks away. But when the day finally arrived, a blizzard made the Chicago sidewalks and roads nearly impassable. Sensing the danger, Craig hesitated to let his son go.

Joey reacted tearfully. "But Dad," he pleaded, "all the other kids will be there! Their parents are letting them go."

Craig thought for a moment, and then replied softly, "All right, I'll let you go."

Surprised but overjoyed, Joey bundled up and plunged into the raging storm. The driving snow made visibility almost impossible, and it took him more than half an hour to trudge the short distance to the party. As he rang the doorbell, he turned briefly to look out into the storm. His eye caught the shadow of a retreating figure. It was his father. He had followed his son's every step to make sure he arrived safely.

Great dads know when to "let go"—and when to follow.

Just Like Daddy's

Children have never been good at listening to their elders,
but they have never failed to imitate them.

JAMES BALDWIN

Brian took his four-year-old young son, Timothy, for a haircut. When the hair stylist asked little Timothy how he'd like his hair to be cut, Timothy's response was, "I want my hair cut just like my daddy's."

Brian beamed and the barber smiled at the father's pride.

Then young Timothy completed his thought: "I want my hair just like daddy's—with a hole on top!"

Children often want to be like Dad—
in good ways and in bad!

Raising a Happy Parent

*Nothing I've ever done has given me more joys
and rewards than being a father to my children.*

BILL COSBY

"Mama, my baby has a heart," Chad announced, over the telephone. "Lucy and I just left the doctor's office. We heard the baby's heartbeat. I cannot believe it!"

Chad's mother grinned. She thought back twenty-eight years earlier to the day that she first heard his heartbeat. The sound was music to her ears and brought joy to her heart. She understood the parental instincts her son was feeling.

She looked forward to the day that his baby—her grandbaby—would come into the world. By the tone of his voice she knew that one day soon, as a parent, her son would better understand that, as parents, our hearts are the happiest when they are beating for our children. Something that doesn't change over twenty-eight years or a lifetime.

The cry of your baby's voice will bring
the sound of music to your ears.

I Love You

A flower cannot blossom without sunshine,
and a man cannot live without love.

GEORGE P. UPTON

"Please God," the young woman asked. "Please let Daddy tell me he loves me today."

Marie's father was terminally ill. Dementia had plagued his mind. He hadn't spoken to her for many weeks.

"I love you, Daddy," she said over and over. Her father simply stared into space. "I love you, Daddy," she whispered once again. "Please say I love you back." Her father wiggled his index finger four times, but didn't say a word.

"Won't you please tell me you love me Daddy?" she begged. Her father wiggled his finger four more times.

"That's what that means," he whispered, as he glanced at his finger and wiggled it several more times. The stunned and grateful daughter was thrilled by her father's final "words" to her.

Sometimes God answers the prayers of His children through the gentle words of a father.

Three in One Year

The most important thing a father can do
for his children is to love their mother.

ANONYMOUS

"You're a very lucky man," the judge announced after the adoption was final. Roy had married the love of his life. Only a couple months into the marriage, he was given the opportunity to adopt his wife's two sons.

Roy realized that he had received a wonderful gift that day. Since these were his first children, he had a lot to learn. But with a smile on his face he wholeheartedly threw himself into raising the boys. Less than a year later, the couple's daughter was born.

"I did something that very few men have accomplished," Roy boasted. "I became the father of three children in less than one year."

In a Father's eyes, three is never a crowd.

The Cat's Meow

A good laugh is sunshine in a house.

WILLIAM MAKEPEACE THACKERAY

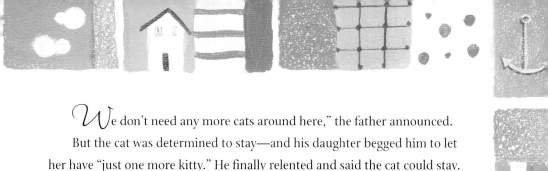

$\mathcal{W}$e don't need any more cats around here," the father announced.

But the cat was determined to stay—and his daughter begged him to let her have "just one more kitty." He finally relented and said the cat could stay.

Nobody could figure out exactly what to call the calico cat. The mom finally looked the cat in the eyes and asked her, "What is your name, cat?"

The cat answered "Meow." So "Meow" became the cat's name right there on the spot.

A few weeks later Meow disappeared. The little daughter was devastated and cried herself to sleep that night. The next morning the entire neighborhood witnessed a funny sight.

The dad was walking around the yard and up and down the street shouting, "Meow. Meow. Meow."

A loving father will do almost anything
to bring a smile to his child's face.

Thank God for Our Sister

Prayer may not change things for you,
but it for sure changes you for things.

SAMUEL SHOEMAKER

The family was busy preparing for the new arrival. The five-year-old twins were convinced that all babies arrived in pairs.

The day Bethany arrived was beautiful. When the family of five met for the first time, Doug smiled at his new little sister. But Dave looked around for the other sister. "Where's my other little sister?" he bawled.

His father tried to explain that not all babies come in twos and that Bethany was the only baby sister God had given them. But Dave wouldn't listen to his dad's words and remained disappointed and inconsolable. So for the next few weeks, he and his brother prayed for another baby sister.

"Thank you, Jesus, for our little sister, but please give us another one, too."

During that time, Bethany kept the family up at night crying. Before long, the twins' prayer changed to "Thank you, Jesus, for our baby sister, and we don't need another one."

God knows exactly what His children
need before they even pray.

A Winning Season

One father is more than a hundred schoolmasters.

GEORGE HERBERT

$\mathcal{U}$nfortunately, the Yellow Jackets, a youth football team, weren't winning any games. Dad was the coach. Mom was the cheerleading sponsor. The boys played on the team. Their little sister was the loudest cheerleader.

The children's grandparents attended all the games, bringing treats and cold drinks along. They became known as the official "team grandparents." Youth football truly became a family affair. And even though the entire family knew that the team just wasn't very good, they enjoyed the season immensely.

During the last game of the season, the boys rallied in the waning seconds of the game to earn their first and only "W" of the year. The players, cheerleaders, parents, grandparents—and of course, coach, who had battled mightily to keep his composure and positive outlook throughout all the losses—jumped up and down, cried, shouted, and celebrated with all the gusto they could muster.

Nine early losses were forgotten. What was remembered was a winning season.

It is not how we start out that makes us smile. It's how we end.

Daddy, I Love You

*Never fear spoiling children by making
them too happy. Happiness is the atmosphere
in which all good affections grow.*

THOMAS BRAY

36

A third-grade teacher assigned her students the task of writing a letter home to their fathers. As she sat at her desk, one of the first she read was this:

"Dear Daddy, I love you so much. When you are going to come see me again? I miss you. When am I going to get to spend the night at your house? Have you ever seen my house before? When am I going to get to see you again? I love you, Daddy."

Four seats away from this letter-writer sat another little girl. Her letter read:

"Dear Dad, I love it when you take me on dates! I like it when you play baseball and miniature golf with me, and take me to movies. I really, really, really like it! I like it when you tell jokes to me, and when you hug and kiss me. Daddy, I love you!"

The teacher sighed as she read the two I love you's and realized how different they were.

*Dads hold such an important place
in their children's lives and hearts.*

The House of Mirrors

*A child is not likely to find a father in God
unless he finds something of God in his father.*

AUSTIN L. SORENSON

I don't think you want to go in there," Daddy said to his little girl. They had been moving from attraction to attraction and ride to ride at a small carnival set up in an abandoned lot near their home.

"But I want to, I want to, I want to," she begged. "Please, Daddy."

"Okay, but be careful," he cautioned.

The little girl walked inside and dashed up to the first couple of mirrors, laughing at the distorted reflections. She saw her Daddy through the glass outside watching her. By the fourth mirror, she had become disoriented, and suddenly wanted to get out—badly. But she couldn't figure out how to escape the glass and chrome maze as she kept hitting dead ends. She finally ran into a pane of glass and burst into tears.

Her father came to the rescue and swept her in his arms. Years later she remembered that he never said, "I told you so," but only spoke the phrase, "I love you."

Our Heavenly Father picks us up
with a smile when we lose our way!

The Perfect Cake

Laughter is the shortest distance between two people.

ANONYMOUS

$\mathcal{M}$ore than anything else that day, the mom wanted her father's birthday cake to be special. Perfect. The problem was her kids were particularly rambunctious as she worked, so she struggled get the cake right.

When her husband returned home from work, he took one look at the cake and began to laugh. Without a word, his wife turned the cake upside down and dropped it in the trashcan. The kids were suddenly very quiet and their dad, now feeling terrible, began to mumble a hasty apology, realizing how hard she had worked.

After another glance at the mess in the trash can, the mom, however, broke the silence with heartfelt laughter. Everyone immediately joined her— her husband in relief—and then all clamored in the minivan to find the perfect cake at the bakery.

The mom decided, at that moment, she didn't have to do everything perfectly for things to be perfect. The dad learned again that you can't laugh at everything—even when the situation is funny to you. And the children learned that words like "I'm sorry" make for happy homes.

A good laugh cannot make an ugly cake pretty—
but it can restore peace to a family.

A Constitutional Privilege

We worry about what a child will be tomorrow,
yet we forget that he is someone today.

STACIA TAUSCHER

Like every other U.S. president before or after him, William Howard Taft had to endure his share of criticism and abuse. One night at the dinner table, his youngest son made a disrespectful remark to him. There was a sudden hush from the other family members. Taft became thoughtful and stroked his chin.

"Well," asked Mrs. Taft, "aren't you going to punish him?"

"If the remark was addressed to me as his father," answered Taft, "he certainly will be punished. However," he continued, "if he addressed it to the President of the United States, then that is his constitutional privilege."

Great dads respect their kids,
remembering that they are people, too.

43

With Skin On

Cherishing children is a mark of civilized society.

JOAN GANZ COONEY

*B*everly attended a weekly Bible study, so on Monday nights, it was Mark's turn to stay home with their four-year-old son, Justin.

The schedule usually ran like clockwork: right after Beverly left, Mark and Justin would have their customary tickle-fest, and then Mark would make sure Justin had his supper and a bath. Then it was story time, after which Mark would kiss Justin's head, tuck him into bed, and head downstairs to watch his favorite TV show at 9 P.M.

But one particular Monday night, two things happened at once to mess up the routine. First, the hero of the TV show was just about to save the day—and second, a terrible thunderstorm blew in, with lightning and loud, booming thunder.

"Dad, I'm scared!" Justin shouted. "Come up here with me!"

"Oh, no," Mark mumbled, gritting his teeth. "Don't worry, Justin," he called out. "You'll be all right. You know God loves you."

"I do know God loves me," cried Justin, "but I need someone with skin on."

Dads are God "with skin on" for their kids.

What Really Matters

The best inheritance a parent can give his
children is a few minutes of his time each day.

O. A. BATTISTA

Reverend Martin was trying to prepare his sermons for Sunday morning—late Saturday afternoon. He had many pressing concerns on his mind, and he was getting frustrated at his inability to concentrate.

Suddenly, he was interrupted by his three-year-old son, Jeremy, who entered his study, sat down at his father's feet, and fixed his big, wondering eyes on his father's face.

Martin turned to him and asked impatiently: "Well? What is it?! What do you want?"

The big, round eyes grew wider still with concern and a little fear. In a little voice he answered hesitantly, "I don't want nuffin; I'se only lookin' at you and lovin' you," instantly melting his dad's heart.

The busy, frustrated minister quickly found that when his heart relaxed—so did his mind and spirit.

Children remind us of what's important in life.

Do As You're Told

Every adult needs a child to teach—
it's the way adults learn.

FRANK A. CLARK

$\mathcal{T}$homas remembers very clearly the time he gave his five-year-old son, Steve, his very first responsibility. He told Steve to watch Susan, his baby sister, while he stepped out of the room.

Thomas had only been gone a few moments when he heard a loud thump, and immediately Susan began to wail.

Thomas rushed back in to find that Susan had fallen from the couch and was lying on the floor, her face red and wet with tears. After checking Susan carefully to be sure she wasn't seriously hurt, Thomas said to his son, "Steve, I told you to watch her!"

"I did!" was Steve's answer. And he was right! He had watched her fall, and he had watched her cry. He had done exactly what he'd been told to do!

Susan wasn't hurt. And Thomas had a great opportunity to work with Steve on the meaning of responsibility.

*Great dads learn how to communicate with their kids—
in ways that their kids can understand!*

49

Dads Are Good for the Soul

Follow my example, as I follow the example of Christ.

1 CORINTHIANS 11:1

Dan and his two children were sitting down in a restaurant. As they bowed their heads, he prayed loudly, "God is good; God is great; thank You for the food; and God, I will thank You even more if Dad gets us ice cream for dessert! Amen."

Along with the laughter from nearby customers, Dan overheard one woman remark equally loudly, "That's what's wrong with this country. Kids today don't even know how to pray. Asking God for ice cream!"

Hearing this, the boy burst into tears and asked his father, "Is God mad at me?"

Dan assured him that he had done a terrific job and that God thought it was a wonderful prayer. Then in a whisper, Dan added, "Too bad that lady never asks God for ice cream. A little ice cream is good for the soul sometimes."

Dan bought his kids ice cream before they left. His son stared at his sundae and then walked over and placed it in front of the woman. With a big smile, he told her, "Here, this is for you. Ice cream is good for the soul sometimes, and my soul is good already!"

Dads' words have a greater influence on their kids than they might think!

Ready to Help

Happy is he that is happy in his children..

ANONYMOUS

A tornado had upset the entire community. No one was injured but many people in the neighborhood had fallen trees and damaged roofs. Ryan was trying to clear the debris in the backyard. He was cutting fallen limbs with his chainsaw. His wife, Jennifer and two-year-old daughter, Anna, were dragging limbs to the street for the city workers to pick up.

The work was hard and no one was saying much. Anna became tired and grew impatient, asking many times when they would be finished. Ryan was too intent on the work at hand to answer.

On a return trip to the backyard, Anna stopped by the garage and what she saw made her eyes light up. She picked up a handheld vacuum cleaner. She proceeded to the backyard, held up the vacuum cleaner and announced to Ryan, who was sweating profusely, "Daddy, I ready to help you now."

No task is too difficult when we take the time to laugh.

Getting the Job Done

True love is but a humble, low-born thing.
It is a thing to walk with hand in hand,
the everydayness of this workaday world.

JAMES RUSSELL LOWELL

The man was attempting to replace the headlight on his car. It was a hot, summer day. He was getting more and more frustrated as he ran into some difficulties, including not having the right screw driver, and a frown settled into his face. His little boy rode his tricycle to the back of the car.

"Hi Daddy!" he shouted. "I love you."

He circled around the car several more times, always shouting the same thing: "Hi Daddy! I love you!"

The man finally stopped what he was doing and reached out to wrestle and tickle with his son for a few seconds. As his little son looked up at him with admiration and gave him a loving smile, his frustration melted.

Before long, the child rode away. His father continued to work on the car. His expression was different, however—his son had left his smile behind. Before long, the job he had dreaded was complete.

A child's smile can make even the most aggravating job more tolerable.

A Father's Love

*"For I know the plans I have for you," declares
the Lord, "plans to prosper you and not to
harm you, plans to give you hope and a future."*

JEREMIAHS 29:11

"*Hey* Bob! Isn't your wife expecting a child?" the teacher asked.

"She was when I left home," Bob replied, looking at the text message on his phone. "But not for much longer."

With those words, he jumped from his desk and took off to the hospital. Bob, unexpectedly a teenage father, had quit high school several years earlier to join the navy to support his family. Now done with his tour of duty, he knew that if he wanted to support his family the way he would like to, he had to finish high school and start college. So Bob was attending high school for a final semester with much younger students—while expecting his second daughter.

When one of his classmates asked if he had any regrets, Bob's answer was: "I have definitely made some mistakes, but I know that my marriage, my children, my love for them, and God's love for me is no mistake at all. And if I have to work a little harder to get established than some men, then I am more than willing to do so. All any of us can do is start right where we are!"

Your family's future begins today!

Family Resemblance

Family faces are magic mirrors. Looking at people
who belong to us, we see the past, present, and future.

Gail Lumet Buckley

$\mathcal{W}$hile studying her five-year-old daughter, Caroline, one evening, a young mother began to entertain a most familiar thought.

"You look just like your Daddy," she said.

It was undeniably evident, with Caroline's flowing dark hair and olive skin. Her eyes were radiantly blue with traces of gold and gray, just like her father's. Her mother, a red-head with fair skin, was jealous of her daughter's flattering features.

But the little girl seemed offended by the remark. Caroline quickly protested, "But I don't want to look like Daddy. I'm a girl!"

(It didn't help that her dad wore a moustache.)

Her mother reassured Caroline that she was indeed beautiful because of her handsome father's imprint on her face. And the mother realized for her own life, as she spoke those words, that every child of God is beautiful for bearing His image.

When people see your face,
may they see your Heavenly Father.

Quality Time

The best thing you can spend on your children is time.

LOUISE HART

During Saturday morning breakfast with his two young daughters, Paul realized that he hadn't been spending as much time with his girls as he would like. After apologizing to them, he said, "You know, it's not always important the quantity of time we spend together, as it is the quality of time we spend together."

Julia, age ten, and Emma, age six, didn't quite understand.

Paul further explained, "Quantity means how much time, and quality means how good the times we spend together are. Which would you rather have?"

Not missing a beat, Julia replied, "Quality time—and a lot of it!"

*One of the most special things about
being a dad is how much your children
need and love lots of time with you!*

Nightlights and Security Blankets

*The best security blanket a child can have
is parents who respect each other.*

JAN BLAUSTONE

One summer evening during a violent thunderstorm, a mother was tucking her small boy into bed. She was about to turn off the light when he asked with a tremor in his voice, "Mommy, will you sleep with me tonight?"

The mother smiled and gave him a reassuring hug. "I can't, Pumpkin," she said, "I have to sleep with your daddy."

A long silence was broken at last by his shaky little voice: "The big sissy."

Dads and moms who make their marriages a priority create strong families and secure children.

The Facts of Life

If you listen carefully to children,
you will have plenty about which to laugh.

STEVE ALLEN

$\mathcal{J}$eremy was in the fifth grade when he heard a number of crude and foul words at school, most dealing with sex. He went home and asked his dad about them. His father responded, "Jeremy, those are bad words that people use to rudely describe something good that God gave us to enjoy."

Like a pro, Jeremy's dad went on to explain the "facts of life." After listening to a detailed explanation of reproduction and the intimacy that occurs between a husband and a wife, Jeremy paused as he digested the information.

Puzzled and shocked, Jeremy, one of seven children, asked his dad only one question at the end: "You mean you and Mom did that seven times?"

Great dads are ready for any
question that comes their way!

Icing on the Cake

This is the day that the Lord has made;
let us rejoice and be glad in it.

PSALM 118:25

$\mathcal{M}$atthew took his two sons, twelve-year-old Kyle and six-year-old David, to his parents' farm for an all-day visit. The sons spent the morning and afternoon helping their grandpa catch up on some overdue chores around the house and barnyard—hammering, lifting, cleaning, feeding, digging, and other heavy labor.

Late that afternoon the four "men" hit the pond, swimming, wrestling, splashing, and having the time of their lives. For dinner, grandma served a classic country meal with two meats, three vegetables, fresh baked breads, and sweetened iced tea. For dessert, it was homemade ice cream melting on warm blackberry cobbler—the boys had picked the blackberries that morning.

As the sun set and it was time to leave, grandma and grandpa hugged their son and grandsons fiercely. "You really made my day, son," Matthew's father said to him.

Six-year-old David quickly piped up, "God made your day, Grandpa—we just put the icing on it."

It's good to be the icing on someone's God-given day!

Home for the Holidays

*When I was a boy of fourteen, my father was so
ignorant I could hardly stand to have the old man around.
But when I got to be twenty-one, I was astonished at
how much the old man had learned in seven years.*

MARK TWAIN

$\mathcal{H}$enry and Sarah were getting up in years, and they hadn't seen their grown children in over a year. Henry decided to call up his son, John, who lived in another part of the country.

"I hate to ruin your day, son," he said, "but your mother and I are divorcing—45 years of misery is enough. We're sick of each other, and I'm sick of talking about this, so you call your sister in Chicago and tell her for us."

Ten minutes later, the phone rang and both John and his sister were on a conference line. "You are not getting divorced! Don't do anything yet! John and I will be there tomorrow!"

Henry hung up the phone and turned to his wife. "Okay," he said, "they're coming for Thanksgiving. Now what do we do about Christmas?"

*Great dads raise their children in such a way
that they enjoy coming home when they are older.*

Let It Rain

A child is a handful some of the time,
but a heartful all of the time.

ANONYMOUS

$\mathcal{R}$ev. Jim Anderson's five-year-old son, Timothy, had been so naughty during the week that his dad decided to give him the worst kind of punishment: he wouldn't be allowed to go to the Sunday school picnic.

When the day came, Jim felt that he had been too harsh on his little son, and so he changed his mind. When he told Timothy that he could go to the picnic after all, the child's reaction was still one of gloom and unhappiness.

"What's the matter? I thought you'd be glad to go to the picnic—you love picnics," Jim said.

"It's too late!" Timothy wailed. "I've already prayed for rain."

Great dads know when to say "no" and when to say "yes."

No Greater Love

*The ultimate test of a man's conscience may be
his willingness to sacrifice something today for future
generations whose words of thanks will not be heard.*

GAYLORD NELSON

Forty-two-year-old David Saunders waited in his driveway for his four-year-old daughter, Danielle, to get off her school bus. A pickup truck was stopped behind the bus. Danielle got off and met her father in the driveway.

Suddenly David noticed a speeding car coming up behind the bus. It swerved to avoid the pickup and, out of control, plunged into the Saunders' driveway. Immediately David grabbed Danielle by the arm and flung her away from himself into the safety of their front yard.

David was struck by the car and pronounced dead at the scene. The sheriff later stated, "It was a heroic act by a father to save his child. He did everything he could, and in the process, he lost his own life. But Danielle owes her life to him."

A father's love is so great he would
give his life for his children.

"Daddy, Please Keep Me From..."

*To us, family means putting your arms
around each other and just being there.*

BARBARA BUSH

Steve bought his two-year-old daughter, Sarah, an aquarium. They went together to the pet store to pick out four fish to put in the tank. One of the fish died a week later—Sarah found it caught in one of the fake plastic bushes.

Sarah's mom called Steve at the office and let Sarah tell the story. In her two-year-old way, she explained that the fish had died, she'd found it in the bushes, and she and Mommy were going to have a funeral in the back yard.

Realizing that this was the first of many losses his daughter would experience in life, Steve comforted Sarah. But he broke into tears at the last thing she said to him before she hung up the phone: "Daddy, please keep me from getting caught in the bushes."

Children need the safety and protection of their dad.

Lifting Weights

The easiest way to convince my kids that they don't really need something is to get it for them.

JOAN COLLINS

$\mathcal{T}$hough skeptical of his son Mark's newfound determination to build bulging muscles, Tom followed his teenager to the store's weight-lifting department, where they admired a set of weights and a bench.

"Please, Dad," Mark pleaded. "I promise I'll use them every day."

"I don't know, Mark," Tom replied. "It's really a commitment on your part."

"Please, Dad?"

"They're not cheap, either," Tom said.

"I'll use them, Dad, I promise. You'll see."

Finally won over, Tom paid for the equipment and headed for the door. After a few steps, he heard Mark behind him say, "What? You mean I have to carry them out to the car?"

Dads often must develop great patience
with their children's pursuits.

Lost Boys

*Our very survival as a nation will depend on
the presence or absence of fathers in the home.*

JAMES DOBSON

$\mathcal{A}$ young man was to be sentenced to the penitentiary. The judge had known him since childhood—he was acquainted with his father, a famous legal mind who had written several seminal books on the law.

"Do you remember your father?" asked the magistrate.

"I remember him well," came the defiant reply.

"As you are about to be sentenced, and as you think of your wonderful dad, what do you remember about him?"

The judge received an answer he did not expect: "I remember that when I went to him for advice, he looked up from his writing and said to me, 'Run along, boy, I'm busy!' Your honor, you remember him as a great man, but I remember him as the father I never knew."

As he passed judgment on the boy, the magistrate sadly muttered to himself: "Alas! Finished the book, but lost the boy."

No matter how great you may be on the outside of the home, what's important is how great you are within the home.

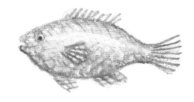

A Father's Fingerprints

Values are like fingerprints. Nobody's are the same,
but you leave them all over everything you do.

ELVIS PRESLEY

When my two-year-old passes by the glass sliding door leading out to our deck, I know he's been there: he's left a mark—several gooey, sticky ones. I desire to leave gooey, sticky, heritage prints, just covering my family. I want them to know I am there, involved, dedicated and loving every moment of it.

After that same two-year-old has given himself a great facial with a lollipop, I'll say to him, "Come here Isaac, you're sticky."

His reply, "I not ticky, I'm keen!" Because he's covered with something pleasant in his mind, he's keen—er, clean.

Let's leave touches that our kids won't want washed off, prints that are pleasant to them—fingerprints of encouragement, of praise, and handfuls of love.

As your children grow, you'll see the many ways your everyday words, smiles, and wisdom impacted them as little ones.

You Are Forgiven and I Love You

What a father says to his children is not heard
by the world, but it will be heard by posterity.

ANONYMOUS

Several years ago, in Spain, a father named Juan had become estranged from his son, Paco. After more than a year spent apart, Juan set off to find his son. He searched for months to no avail.

In a last, desperate effort to find him, the father put a full page ad in a Madrid newspaper. It read: Dear Paco, meet me in front of this newspaper office at noon on Saturday. You are forgiven. I love you. Your father.

On Saturday, 800 different young men named Paco showed up, all seeking forgiveness and love from their fathers.

Children crave their fathers' acceptance and love.

Daddy's Jokes

*Having a young child explain something
exciting he has seen is the finest example
of communication you will ever hear or see.*

BOB TALBERT

A grandmother was tucking her granddaughter into bed one evening when the child remarked, "Mommy and Daddy are entertaining some very important people downstairs."

"You're right," agreed the grandmother. "Did your mommy or daddy tell you about the people?"

"No, but they did tell me that I had to be real good and real quiet tonight."

"So is that how you knew that the guests are real important?" the grandmother asked with a smile.

"Nope. All you have to do is listen," advised her granddaughter. "Mommy is laughing at all of Daddy's jokes."

When moms and dads delight in one another,
the children are at peace in the world.

85

Congratulations to You, Sir

You don't raise heroes; you raise sons.
And if you treat them like sons, they'll turn out
to be heroes, even if it's just in your own eyes.

WALTER SCHIRRA, SR.

*I*t was the decade following the Great Depression. The president of the corporation stepped up to the platform, accompanied by an overall-clad man off the assembly line, and made this speech:

"Ladies and gentlemen, you are about to see how American industry rewards those who are conscientious and hard-working. This man standing beside me has been with the company less than a year, during which time his unusual qualities have caught my attention. I've watched him closely, observed with great pleasure the manner in which he has pitched in and gotten things done. I am pleased to announce that starting this very afternoon, he gets out of his work clothes, comes into the executive branch, and takes over an office with the title of Vice President at an annual salary of eighty thousand dollars. Congratulations to you, sir."

The workman shook the extended hand and said: "Gee, thanks, Dad."

Great dads do everything they can
to see their children succeed!

The Small Things of God

In God's sight there are no little people and no little places.

FRANCIS SCHAEFFER

On one summer vacation in North Carolina, my daughter was swimming in the surf and lost a favorite bracelet. After searching and coming up empty handed, she was devastated. We talked and prayed about God's love for her, even in the small things. We left the beach for lunch and left the bracelet in God's hands.

Later we returned for a walk and as my daughter was looking for shells, I went to put my feet in the water. As I entered the waves, guess what rolled up between my feet? I picked up the once lost but now found treasure and called to my daughter. Imagine the joy of a "little thing" being placed back into the care of her hands while learning an invaluable lesson about the small things of God.

Nothing—no dad nor child—
is too small to escape God's attention.

Questioning God

Every single act of love bears the imprint of God.

ANONYMOUS

$\mathcal{M}$y son Mike asks some great questions. He once asked, "Why do bats hang upside down?"

I earnestly sought out the answer for him, surfing the web and all the bat sites I could read. I learned more about bats than I ever planned on knowing—I certainly never thought I would know that an infant bat weighs one-third as much as its mother at birth.

I went to the lengths I did to satisfy Mike's curiosity because of my love for him. More than just knowing why bats hang upside down, I wanted my son to know that his father cared about his questions.

Most of all I wanted him to understand that my desire to know him reflects how the Heavenly Father feels about us—He invites questions that lead to a greater understanding of Him and His will for us.

When we love our children as extravagantly
as God loves us, he is pleased.

One Summer Day

Home is the first school and the first church
where we learn about loving God.

ERNESTINE SCHUMANN-HEINK

$\mathcal{M}$y two oldest sons and I drove to the swimming hole one hot summer day. After the boys tumbled out of the car and ran into the lake, I watched as they encountered a kid named Jack, who was struggling with venturing from the shallow end to a floating dock at the deep end.

My boys swam over to Jack and made friends within minutes. They convinced him to make the swim he was deliberating—they knew he could do it and they would swim alongside him just to be safe and wouldn't it be cool to jump off the dock? With their cajoling, Jack finally stroked his way out of the shallow end.

When Jack and my boys reached the dock, they celebrated riotously at Jack's accomplishment and swam back ashore to tell their tale.

I was so proud to realize that my sons were modeling what I had tried to model for them: that we need each other to help us along and celebrate life's victories.

When we teach our children the ways
of the Kingdom, they in turn pass it on to others.

Pause for a Commercial Break

The word "engagement" has two meanings:
in war, it's a battle; in courtship, a surrender.

AUTHOR UNKNOWN

It was time to ask my girlfriend's father for her hand in marriage. He and I were watching TV on the couch. I wasn't about to bother him during the game, so I had to wait for a commercial. But every time a commercial would come on, my heart would start beating wildly in my chest, my breath would get short, and by the time I had worked up enough nerve to ask him, the game would be back on.

Finally, I stood up and walked over to him—but I was too slow again, and the game had resumed.

I was already standing there like an idiot, so I knelt down like I had to tie my shoe. After a while, Mr. Conway said, "Mike, is there something I can do for you?"

I looked up and said something like, "I...uh...I would-like-to-marry-your-daughter-if-that-is-okay-with-you. I-love-your-daughter-and-would-take-care-of-her."

He looked down at me, smiled, and told me he would like that. Then he patted me on the head—and went back to the game. I felt the weight of the world lift off my shoulders.

The best dads are the ones who do what is best for their wives—and their daughters.

A Prayer for a Dad's Heart

Be strong and courageous. Do not be afraid or terrified because of them, for the LORD your God goes with you; he will never leave you nor forsake you.

DEUTERONOMY 31:6

Dear Heavenly Father,

I pray that you will mold me into the strong and courageous father that You want me to be. Grant me the wisdom I need to raise children who are confident and caring. Help me to be an example of faith and love to them. Thank You for the gift of my children.